Grace Goes Bowhunting

By Shasta Sitton

Illustrated by Marvin Teeples

Whitetail Press, LLC

Copyright © 2014 Shasta Sitton

ISBN 978-0-9915571-2-7

"Mom and Dad, can we go shoot our bows?"
Grace asks. "I really want to practice one more
time before we go hunting in the morning."
"Sure!" Mom replies. "Let's go!"

They grab their bows and head to the backyard.

Grace starts out shooting at 20 yards, then 25, then 30! She hits close to the bullseye every time at 20 and 25 yards, but keeps missing at 30.

"Darn!" says Grace. "If I'm not consistent at 30 yards, what am I going to do if the deer is that far away?"

"You'll have to let it go," Dad replies. "For now, 30 yards is too far for you. You'd be more likely to miss or injure the deer. But you're great at 20 and 25 yards!"

"And we'll be there to help you," Mom adds with a smile.

The next morning,
Mom and Dad wake
Grace up so early
she can still see the
moon in the dark sky.
Grace is very tired and
wants to go back to
sleep…but wait! She
suddenly remembers that
she's going hunting today!
She leaps out of bed to get
dressed.

When everyone is ready,
they climb in Dad's truck
and head to the woods.

"Alright, we're here," says Dad as he stops the truck. "Grace, you're going to be hunting with Mom today. I'll be just up the road in a tree stand. Good luck!"

"Thanks, Dad. See you soon," Grace replies as she climbs out of the truck.

As Dad drives away, Grace realizes how dark it still is. She is very glad her mom is with her. She watches as her mom gets her headlamp out of her backpack and puts it on. Grace quickly does the same.

"Now we need to spray ourselves with scent free spray," Mom says. "Since we're bowhunting, we're going to be very close to the deer. The spray will make it harder for the deer to smell us."

Mom and Grace spray each other, their gear, and their boots.

"You ready?" Mom asks.

"Yep! Let's go!" Grace replies confidently even though she is a little nervous.

"Remember to walk as quietly as you can so we don't scare any deer away," Mom reminds her.

Grace shivers in the chilly morning. She didn't realize it would be so cold... or noisy. There are owls hooting, coyotes yipping, and lots of frogs croaking.

Grace is listening so intently that she nearly runs right into her mom, who is stopped in front of their deer blind. They quietly climb in the blind, and sit on their stools.

Mom opens the blind windows in front of them. "Go ahead and nock an arrow in your bow," Mom says. "That way you'll be ready to shoot if we see a deer."

Grace nocks an arrow,
then they both try to be
as still and quiet as possible.
Outside, the sky slowly
turns from black, to violet,
to blue, as the sun rises
higher and higher.

"Now," Mom whispers, "we'll use the rangefinder to see how far away some of the trees are. That way, if you see a deer near one of those trees, you'll have a better idea of how far away it is."

Grace uses the rangefinder to see which trees are 20 and 25 yards away.

A short while later, Mom uses her grunt call to try to get any deer that are close by to come even closer. The call makes a strange, deep noise.

Grace is on the edge of her seat searching for any sign of deer. Tree. Tree. Rock. Tree. Deer! "Mom, look!" Grace whispers excitedly as she points to the deer. Her mom looks through her binoculars to get a closer look.

"It's a doe," Mom whispers back.
"You have a buck tag, so we're going
to have to let the doe go. Good job
spotting her though! Keep it up!"

Grace goes back to searching the woods.
Time passes slowly, and she feels her
eyelids getting heavier and heavier.
She figures it wouldn't hurt to close her eyes
for just a minute. Just as her eyes start to close,
she feels a tap on her leg.
"Grace, look!" Mom whispers. "There's a buck."
Grace jerks up. She sees a buck through the
trees. She slowly begins to raise her bow.

wait," whispers Mom. "He's still 40 yards away. We need to wait for him to get closer." "But, Mom," Grace replies, "what if he never comes closer? Can't I just try?"

"No," Mom replies. "You need to make the best shot you can so you kill the deer, not just injure it. Go ahead and stand up. Get your bow ready, but don't draw until he's closer."

Mom uses her grunt call again. The deer lifts his head, and starts to strut closer.

"Get ready," Mom whispers.

Grace's heart is beating so loud she's afraid the deer will hear it. She watches the deer as he gets closer and closer.

Mom looks through the rangefinder again. "Ok, he's at 25 yards," Mom whispers so quietly Grace can barely hear her. "Wait until he looks away from us, so he doesn't see you draw your bow. Once he's broadside, shoot him right behind the shoulder blade."

Grace stands as still as possible. When the deer steps behind a tree, she quickly draws her bow and waits. As soon as he steps out from behind the tree, she takes a deep breath, and slowly squeezes her release.

Thwack. The arrow being released barely makes a sound. She sees the deer jump in the air, and run into the trees.

"I hit it!" says Grace excitedly. "Let's go get it!"

"Hold on," replies Mom. "Let's give it some time. We saw which way it went, and you made a good shot. It should be easy to track if we don't scare it further away."

A short while later, Mom and Grace quietly climb out of the blind. They walk to the spot where the deer was hit, and find a few spots of blood on the ground. A few feet away is her arrow with evidence of a good shot.

"See the blood?" Mom asks. "This is from your deer. We're going to follow the blood until we find him."

They slowly walk forward. Every now and then, Mom stops to show her more blood. They follow the spots further and further. Grace starts to feel nervous that they won't find the deer. Maybe her shot wasn't as good as she thought.

Just then, Grace sees antlers sticking up from behind a fallen log. It's the buck!

"Mom, look!" Grace exclaims. "There he is!"

"Is he dead?" Grace asks as they slowly walk closer. Mom bends down to look. "Yes, he is," Mom replies. "Congratulations, Grace! You just harvested your first deer! I'm so proud of you."

Grace suddenly feels a rush of emotions; excitement, pride, and a little bit of sadness that the buck is dead. She says a silent thank you to the deer for giving its life to feed her family.

"Mom, that was amazing!" Grace says. "Thank you for taking me hunting. I can't wait to go again."

A week later, Grace and her family sit down for dinner. They are eating venison steaks from her buck.

All of the time spent practicing with her bow was well worth it. She can't wait for her next hunting adventure.

The End.
(How many deer
can you find in
this picture?)

My First Deer

Place a picture here of your first deer
and write your story below

_____

_____

_____

_____

_____

_____